ABOUT THE BOOK

It was Christmas Day when the Pilgrims began work on the Plymouth settlement, but the feasting and caroling of the traditional English holiday seemed forgotten. Giles saw real hatred in the sailors' eyes. They were angry with their passengers because of the weeks taken to explore Cape Cod for a good sheltered harbor. Every day in the New World made the winter seas more dangerous for the ship's return to England.

Captain Christopher Jones took the Pilgrims' part. Even with food supplies low aboard the *Mayflower*, the women and children would live aboard ship until shelter ashore could be built. When Giles left the ship with the men and boys to work on the Common House, his little sister Damaris made him promise to bring back "something to make Christmas."

At the end of the day, Giles brought greens from the forest to deck the tables, and birch branches to make stick horses for the small children. He was not the only one who'd thought of Christmas. On the beach were five wild geese and several smaller waterfowl. There was an iron kettle of white clams, and a split hollow log filled with wild honey. Giles felt his stomach turn with delight.

That evening on board ship, some of the Pilgrims disapproved of the Christmas festivities and the sailors were on the verge of mutiny; but at the Captain's request, all men forgot their quarrels with one another as they sat down to Christmas dinner together.

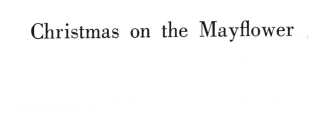

Christmas on the Mayflower

CHRISTMAS ON
THE MAYFLOWER

BY WILMA PITCHFORD HAYS
ILLUSTRATED BY ROGER DUVOISIN

Coward-McCann, Inc.
New York

For Maynard, Beulah, Marjorie, Georgia
and Virginia

AT DUSK Giles Hopkins walked the deck of the *Mayflower*. Tomorrow would be Christmas and he was to go on shore and help build the Pilgrims' first shelter, the Common House. But he would not mind working on Christmas Day if he could leave this ship.

When he first boarded the *Mayflower* more than three months ago, he had loved the mixture of smells from her old cargoes—wine and tar, timber and turpentine. Now he was sick of everything about the ship. He never wanted to hear again the creak of her timbers as she groaned through stormy seas. He was tired of the stuffy cabin where a hundred and two Pilgrim passengers crowded together.

As Giles reached the forecastle, where the crew of thirty sailors lived, he heard voices raised in a quarrel.

Most of all I'll be glad to be away from these rough men, Giles thought. From the first, the sailors had made fun of their hymn-singing, praying passengers. For days now, Giles had seen real hatred in their eyes. The crew wanted to sail for England. Each day of delay brought winter closer and made their voyage more dangerous.

Giles knew why the sailors were angry. The Pilgrims had explored Cape Cod for six weeks before they voted to make their new home at sheltered Plymouth Harbor.

Giles heard one of the sailors shout, "We've wasted enough time on these fool Pilgrims. You want to freeze and starve with them?"

"No!" the men cried.

A loud voice sounded above the others. "I say, dump them on land and head back to England before our food gives out."

Captain Jones wouldn't do that, Giles thought.

Neither would the first mate, Clarke, nor the pilot, Robert Coffin. But what if these officers couldn't control the angry sailors?

The forecastle grew quiet. Perhaps the crew were making whispered plans. Giles shivered.

Now he could hear no sound except the slapping of the waves against the ship. A mile and a half away on shore, he saw patches of snow. Beyond was the dark forest. There were no lighted windows anywhere as there were in the English countryside where he had lived.

We are the only people in this wilderness, he thought, except for savages. We must do everything ourselves with the tools we have brought and what we can find here.

A hand touched his arm.

"Damaris," he said to his little sister, "what are you doing here at the sailor's end of the deck?"

"*You* are here," she said. "Besides, I brought you some supper."

Giles took the hard biscuit and cheese she held

out to him. How good it would be to eat hot food in a home again. On the *Mayflower* the Pilgrims cooked in iron kettles swung over a charcoal fire built on a sandbox on deck. Often stormy weather made even this simple cooking impossible. Only the crew had hot meals cooked in the galley under the forecastle. The store of food for the crew was kept separate from the Pilgrims' scanty provisions.

Again the muttering of the sailors grew loud. Giles recognized the voice of the tough old Bosun, whose language shocked the Pilgrims when he shouted at the sailors in the rigging.

Damaris trembled and took her brother's hand.

"Come," he said, walking with her toward the stern. "Pull your shawl closer."

How little her hand was in his. She was very small to have endured so much cold and danger. Through storm after storm as the ship pitched and rolled he had held Damaris in her bunk while their mother held tightly to the new baby,

Oceanus. They would have been crushed if they had been thrown to the floor, where great boxes and sea chests slid back and forth across the cabin. Even so, they had been safer than the men who had to sleep between decks or in the hold.

"Think of it, Damaris," he said. "We will soon have homes again. We begin to build to-morrow and I am to help."

For a moment Damaris did not answer. When she did, she sounded as if she wanted to cry but would not. "Do you know what day tomorrow is, Giles?"

"Monday, of course," he said. "For if this weren't Sunday, we'd be ashore working."

"You're just like the men! Even Mother and the other women think only of the houses and getting ashore to wash our clothes in fresh brook water. No one cares that tomorrow is Christmas."

In the dim light, Giles saw Damaris' lips tremble and tears come to her blue eyes.

"I thought of it," he said gently, "but I didn't

talk about it. What good would it do to remember—this year? Half the people on board don't celebrate Christmas. Master Bradford says it is a day of frivolous excitement."

"But our family doesn't believe that," Damaris cried. "Remember our last Christmas in England? There was a big yule log in the fireplace. And a feast, with everyone eating together, even the servants and the men who worked in the fields. Remember how we sang carols, Giles? And father brought me a doll with golden hair—but now she is washed overboard."

Giles remembered. At sea, mountains of waves had washed across the decks, springing open the cabin doors, carrying away clothing and pots before the men could fasten the door again. Damaris and her little friend, Remember, had lost their dolls.

"I don't mind for myself," Giles said. "A new place is exciting and I shall be going ashore with the men. But I wish I had something for you, Damaris. How did you know what date it is?"

"Constance told us. On deck today she told all the children stories while Mother was caring for the sick in the cabins. Constance remembers everything, Giles. The smell of pudding boiling in the kitchen. Roast goose and pig turning on the spit. The wassail bowl steaming with ginger and cinnamon."

"Don't!" Giles groaned.

He wished his sister Constance had not brought back these memories to the smaller children, but maybe she was homesick and wanted to remember the way they had lived in England.

"Damaris," he said suddenly, "tomorrow I'll find something to bring to you when I come back to the ship."

"For Constance, too? Will you bring her something for Christmas?"

"I'll try," Giles said.

There was a sound on the poop deck above. Giles looked up to see the straight square shoulders of Captain Christopher Jones.

"Good evening, sir," Giles said.

"Captain Jones," Damaris cried. "Giles has promised to bring back something to make Christmas tomorrow."

The gray-haired man looked down at them. In the darkness they could not see his face under the brimmed cap, but his voice was kind.

"I was thinking, too, of the yuletide, and how my family will be celebrating it tomorrow in England. The feasting and the children."

He stopped, then said good night, and went back into the poop house.

Quietly Giles and Damaris went to the cabin and to bed.

The next morning Giles woke in the darkness of the cabin. He was too excited to remember anything but that the shallop sailed for shore at dawn. He stumbled up the steps of the narrow companionway under the quarter-deck. Already men were clustered at the rail.

Leaning over the side, Giles took hold of the heavy rope ladder hanging above the shallop. It seemed a long way down to the small boat

the Pilgrims had brought with them, stowed under the spar deck of the *Mayflower*.

The shallop, bobbing on the water, was rapidly filling with Pilgrim men. As Giles started down the swinging ladder, Damaris ran and threw her arms around his neck and whispered in his ear.

"Don't forget, something to make Christmas. You promised."

Constance leaned over the rail. "Giles, bring some pine from the forest. We can deck the tables. That, at least, will be like home."

Someone shouted, "Hurry there," and Giles dropped into the shallop. From below, the double-decked *Mayflower* looked larger than she had when he was on board. Under the water he could see the dim shape of her great hold, which he knew had three levels for cargo, stowage, water casks and sail lockers.

Giles waved to Damaris. He saw the boys who were too young to go—Love and Wrestling Brewster, Francis Billington, John Cooke, Joseph

Mullins and Resolved White. They were looking down at him enviously, and he waved again to them.

With Thomas English at the helm, the shallop moved slowly away from the *Mayflower* and her prow stood in to shore. The boat skimmed over water too shallow for the big *Mayflower,* heading for the wide mouth of the brook that emptied into the harbor. Giles crowded to the bow, breathless with wonder.

He had seen this brook pictured on the map his father and the other Pilgrim men had bought from Captain John Smith before they left England. He had even seen the bushy-bearded John Smith talking to the Pilgrims when he offered to come with them.

John Smith knew this land well. Alone in an open boat, he had sailed the two thousand miles of coast about ten years ago. He had mapped it all and his map was true. He had even named this harbor Plymouth years before the Pilgrims came.

But the Pilgrims had already hired a soldier

captain, Miles Standish. Giles' father had said that the men thought it cheaper to buy Captain John Smith's map than to hire him to guide them.

Yet I wish Captain Smith were here, Giles thought. He loved this land from the moment he saw it. He told us he did. And I feel the same way. The air is cold but the sky is wonderfully blue. Already I smell the pines, and there's the marsh where Father says we can cut reeds and grass to thatch the roofs of our houses.

From the boat Giles could not see the berry bushes, the wild leeks and the onions which his father had said would be ready to eat in the spring. He couldn't see the sassafras which Master Fuller was so happy to find because he prescribed it as a tea for almost every sickness.

But clearly now Giles saw the banks of clay, the sand and the stone to be used with the trees for building.

"I will never cry for our old Christmases if I can explore a land like this," he said excitedly to his father as they stood together in the prow of

the shallop. "It is wonderful to be here even if it isn't like home."

Elder Brewster turned to him. "You are right, Giles. This is a fair land. With God, we shall feel at home in any place."

The shallop pulled near the shore where a great boulder ran out into the water. Above, on a bluff, Giles saw the men who had been left on shore Saturday to guard the spot chosen for their first building, the Common House.

Edward Dotey was there. Edward was one of the eleven young men whom the Pilgrims had hired to work for several years in payment for their passage to this new world. He worked for Giles' father. Giles liked him, even if he did tease.

"Edward, I've come to help," Giles called, as he jumped over the gunwale and splashed ashore.

As Giles scrambled up the side of the bluff, Edward reached down his big hand and helped him. "Maybe you wouldn't have come, if you knew we heard the cries of savages in the forest last night."

"Indians?" Giles said. "Did they hurt anyone?"

"Didn't even see them," Edward said. "At the first alarm, we shot off a musket. After that there wasn't a sound, though we sat up far into the night and watched."

Giles knew that Indians had lived here at Plymouth. When the men first went ashore several days ago, they had found cleared fields where rotted stalks of Indian corn lay. But there were no Indian homes. The place seemed deserted. These Indian fields had been one of the reasons for choosing this spot to settle. The soil was good. The land was already cleared for spring planting.

"I'm not afraid of Indians," Giles said. "Come, let's help Father."

The men were gathered on the north bank of the brook, just above the beach. They carried axes and saws, hatchets and knives. They were ready to lay the foundations of their Common House.

Francis Eaton, shipbuilder and carpenter, was

directing the work. "Measure her off careful, twenty feet square, exact," he said.

He's planned the Common House the same size as the ship's cabin, Giles thought. That won't be big enough. We're terribly crowded on the ship. Then he remembered that the Common House was only the first of their buildings. Later they would put up houses in a row leading up the hill.

"Giles," his father called. "We'll work in pairs. You take this hatchet and trim the branches from the trees Edward cuts down. Be sure to chop close to the trunk."

The men set to work. Around him Giles heard the ring of axes, the snarl of saws and the crack of trees being riven in the sharp winter air.

It seemed to him that each tree Edward cut had more branches than the one before. Giles chopped and chopped. When his legs became tangled in loose boughs, he had to stop and clear a space in which to work. But the white and gold birch bark and the green pine were beautiful. The

smell of the fresh-cut wood was pleasant, too.

Giles looked at the long straight tree trunks he had trimmed and piled on the ground. Soon men would come and split them into thick planks to build the Common House. He was so proud of his share in the building that he almost forgot his scratched arms and the blisters on his hands.

At last, when the sun was overhead, Edward and Giles stopped work to go to the spring for water. They followed an Indian trail to the sandy beach at the edge of the brook. Giles went down on his knees to drink the bubbling water. It tasted so wonderfully sweet that he drank and drank until he had to stop for breath.

"I wish I could take some of the water to Mother and Constance and Damaris," he said. "After that brackish water we've had on ship all these months, this would be a grand present."

"We've nothing to carry it in," Edward said. "It would slop out of an open kettle when the shallop rolls in the waves."

Giles told Edward about his promise to his sisters.

"It will be easy to gather the greens Constance wants," he said. "We can take armfuls of the trimmings from the trees. But what can I take to Damaris?"

He was still trying to think of something that afternoon when his father sent him with Edward into the swamp to cut reeds and marsh grass and tie them into bundles of thatch.

"If I had the knife Father promised me for my birthday, I could carve trenchers from wood. Damaris and Remember like to play house with small dishes. But my old knife is too dull for such fine whittling. I remember Father carved me a head for a stick horse once. I rode it everywhere as if it were a real horse."

He paused. "You know, Edward, one of those straight branches we cut from the birch trees would make a fine stick horse. I could notch the end and tie a bright ribbon from Mother's sea chest for reins. Damaris would like that. And there are lots of branches. We can take back enough for all the youngest children."

"The women won't thank you for having a herd of wild horses running over the ship all day tomorrow," Edward laughed.

Giles saw something else growing at the edge of the swamp. He ran to the tall bushes with branches heavy with red berries.

"We can cut armfuls of these. With greens the berries will look like holly," he shouted.

In late afternoon Edward and Giles returned to the place above the beach where the men were building the Common House. The foundations were already laid.

Edward carried the branches of red berries to the shallop. From scattered boughs of pine, Giles hacked out a dozen tough knots oozing with resin. He would give these to his mother to make a bright fire by which to sew or read.

When he came puffing to the edge of the water with his armfuls of greens and birch branches, he found that he was not the only one who had thought of Christmas. On the sand were five wild geese and several smaller waterfowl. There was an iron kettle filled with white clams. Giles felt his stomach turn with anticipation.

And there was a yule log. It was not as large as those which blazed in the great fireplaces at home, but placed on sandboxes end to end on the deck of the *Mayflower,* it would make a bright fire.

Giles looked down at the sandy beach and saw that the tide had brought in some shells. They had beautiful scalloped edges. Their cupped inner sides were pink or gold or pearly gray. Damaris would love these. She could use them for play dishes, or just look at them because they were so pretty.

Then Master Mullins and John Alden came with part of a split hollow log packed with wild honey.

This is a good Christmas to take to the ship, Giles thought. Honey for our hard biscuits. Clams and fowl. A yule log. Red berries and greens to deck our table. All these shells and stick horses for the children.

The shallop was being loaded now. Giles

climbed on deck from the boulder. Those men who had no children or wives on the ship had offered to remain on guard this Christmas night. A big goose was left for them and a chunk of honey in the comb.

The men were still working by the light of a fire as the shallop pulled away from the shore. Giles waved to Edward and John Howland and Master Winslow.

When the shallop came alongside the *Mayflower,* it was almost dark. Giles was the first one up the ladder. He wanted to see his little sister's face when she saw all they had brought back.

But as he dropped onto the *Mayflower* deck, he felt a queer silence. Then he saw the sailors knotted three deep against the mainmast. By the flickering charcoal fire from the sandboxes, he saw their scowling faces. Facing them across the fire huddled the Pilgrim women and children. No one moved. Little Dog, the spaniel the children loved, pressed against Damaris' ankles.

Captain Jones stood a little above the others on

a thick coil of rope. He seemed to be facing both groups at once. His mouth was tight and straight.

"What is this?" Giles heard his father say behind him.

All the Pilgrim men were aboard now. Carrying wild fowl and greens, they crossed the deck and stood beside the women.

Giles felt a tingle go down his spine as the sailors shuffled and glared, but did not speak. He could hear nothing except the creak of the ship pulling against the three great anchors which had been left down since Friday's heavy storm.

Then he saw Damaris' white face as she knelt to put her arm around Little Dog. Giles' cheeks grew hot. What had these rough men been doing to frighten his sisters and mother and all the other women and children? Even Little Dog was afraid.

A thin-faced sailor in the front row shouted, "Those psalm singers will have no food from the crew's store, even on Christmas. We've little enough to last us back to England."

"He's right," a thick-necked sailor cried. "I'm

for dumping the whole lot of them ashore to-night—and pulling out in the morning. There's nothing to stop us."

Giles saw Captain Jones catch up a heavy boat hook. He stood holding it easy in his hand, but his eyes looked as if they were on fire.

"I'll not abandon Englishmen to die," he said. "We stay here so these women and children can live on the ship until their homes are built. Even if we have to go on short rations ourselves.

"And we'll share the raisin porridge the cook has boiled—yes, and our cask of strong water, too."

The sailors muttered. One showed yellowed teeth like an angry dog.

Giles' throat felt thick. Then he saw that, for all their rebellion, the crew still knew who was Captain on the *Mayflower*.

A feeling of thankfulness filled Giles. The sailors had spoken the truth. The *Mayflower* could leave at any time. Everyone knew that Captain Jones understood the danger of remaining longer.

He wanted to sail at once. He had told the Pilgrims how foolish it was to try to settle this land in winter. He had even offered to take them back to England without payment, but they had refused. Still, Captain Jones would not desert them.

Giles heard the women talking to the Pilgrim men. Their faces showed no fear now. They were angry. One of the men spoke to Captain Jones.

"We thank you for your offer of porridge from the ship's store. But we will do with what we have. We have no wish to eat with these ruffians."

Then it was the Pilgrims' turn to feel the Captain's sharp words. "Everyone on this ship will share the Christmas meal together—or no one will cook anything," he said. "Have you forgotten what is said each Christmas in England over the yule log?"

The eyes of each person went to the thick log which had been dropped on the deck when the men sensed there was trouble.

Captain Jones spoke quietly. He lifted his hand

with the iron hook as if he were lifting the cup in Old England.

"This yule log burns. It destroys all old hatreds and misunderstandings. Let your envies vanish. Let the spirit of good fellowship reign through the season and through the year."

Giles remembered these words from other years. The lowliest beggar coming to an English door this season would be treated as well as a prince. And no one could sit down to Christmas dinner until he had forgiven his enemies.

Some of the Pilgrims seemed ashamed as the Captain waited. The sailors looked more thoughtful, too.

Then, as if he couldn't bear the strange silence, Little Dog frisked from under Damaris' skirts. He ran from one group to the other, wagging his tail. He was comical, as if he were trying to say, "Didn't you hear the good Captain? Let us all be friends and burn the yule log together."

Giles laughed. Some of the Pilgrims smiled. They nodded their heads at Captain Jones. The men went to finish unloading the shallop. Even the sailors returned to work without any more grumbling.

Later, while the yule log burned brightly on the boxes of sand, Giles notched all the birch branches with their white or golden bark. Through these notches, the children tied red or blue or green ribbons the women had given from their sea chests. For Damaris' horse, Giles made a fringed tail from a piece of worn red shawl.

While they worked in the light of the flames, the children sang together. Giles found it hard to follow the twisted words of the hymn Love and Wrestling Brewster knew so well.

> Thou Makest fat mine head with oincting oil;
> My cup abounds, doubtless good and mercie
> Shal all the dayes of my life folow me;
> Also in Jehovah's howse, I shal
> To length of dayes, repose me quietlie.

But Giles sang lustily on the carol:

> Come along with noise
> My merrie merrie boys
> The Christmas log to the firing.

On your Psalteries play,
That sweet luck may
Come while the log is trending.

At last the children heard a call from between decks. The food was ready. As they pushed down the stairs, Giles saw the happiness in Damaris' eyes and he smiled.

The wooden tables had been brought together. They were scrubbed until each board shone with cleanliness. Down the center of the tables were pine and red berries and candles. Wooden trenchers were set out with the best pewter from the sea chests.

A place was laid for every person on the ship except those who were ill. Giles could see the women carrying bowls of porridge for them to the cabin. Even those who did not believe in a frivolous Christmas were at the table. They saw no harm in celebrating the laying of the foundation of their Common House on this day.

"Look, Giles," Damaris said. "There are the babies, too, in their cradles. Constance is singing

to them."

Giles went over to look at his baby brother, Oceanus, and at Peregrine White, the first child born after the Mayflower reached Cape Cod six weeks ago. Constance, rocking a cradle on each side of her, cautioned Giles to be quiet. She sang the warning right in the middle of the lullabye.

> "Sh-h-h. Don't wake the babies.
> We want them to sleep
> So everyone can eat.
>
> "Lul-lay, thou little tiny Child
> By, by, lully, lullay.
> Lullay, thou little tiny Child,
> By, by, lully, lullay."

The meal was soon finished. Not a mouthful remained of the clams, the fowl, or the raisin porridge the cook had made. Giles could not say that he was exactly full. But honeycomb and hard biscuits were being passed with steaming cups which smelled of cinnamon from the Captain's sea chest. The meal had begun in strained silence, but food and the children's laughter had made everyone

feel more friendly. They began to talk.

A sailor with leathery skin and one eye bandaged sat next to Giles. He took a sprig of pine from the table and sniffed it.

"We always had pine when I was a boy," he said.

Giles found it hard to think of this man with the tough knotted hands as a boy.

"In my country they tell a tale of the pine," the sailor went on. "They say an old pine tree dropped its branches down around the Holy Family to hide them from Herod's soldiers. And when the danger was past, the Christ Child blessed the old pine—so all pine carries his blessing yet."

Giles sat looking at the sprig of pine turning in the brown fingers. He could scarcely believe that these words came from one of the men who had faced Captain Jones a few hours ago.

Across the table was another sailor with thick black hair and a knife scar down his cheek. "I say a candle must burn all night," he said. "In Ire-

land we keep a candle burning so the Christ Child will never have to search again for a home to enter. And only a girl named Mary shall blow it out in the mornin'."

Everyone looked at Mary Chilton and she blushed.

Down the table, nearer Damaris and Constance, Giles saw a tall man whose roughened skin was darker than his blond hair. He had saved his biscuit.

"To fix in the riggin' for the birds," he said for everyone to hear. "In Norway, we tie sheaves of grain outside our windows for the birds on Christmas Day."

Only the tough Bosun had not joined in the talk. He sat at the end of the table, alone and scowling. Giles saw Damaris look at the man several times. He knew she wanted everyone to be happy at this Christmas meal. Then he saw her leave her place. With Little Dog trotting at her heels, she went to the end of the table. Under her arm she carried the stick horse Giles had made for her. She stopped beside the Bosun.

He did not look at her. She touched his sleeve and said something. The man turned on her with such a frown that Giles half rose from the table to go to his sister.

Then he saw Damaris smile. She climbed on her stick horse and galloped around in a circle as if she wished to show the Bosun how fast she could ride. Little Dog chased after the red wool tail. He barked so excitedly that everyone turned to look.

The little girl rode faster and faster. Little Dog seemed about to catch his own tail as he tried to keep up with her. Pilgrims and sailors laughed together. The scowl left the Bosun's face. For a moment he looked almost pleasant.

Then Captain Jones stood at the head of the table and gave the last toast. Each person stood, even the Bosun.

"Everywhere this night may there be fire to warm the cold, food for the hungry, rest for the weary. And may all enjoy Heaven's peace."

As the people left the tables, Damaris ran to walk with Giles. They were on deck on their way to the cabin before he remembered the shells in his pockets.

"Damaris," he said. "I brought you something else."

He put a shell in her hand. She could not see its scalloped beauty, but she felt the inside.

"It's smooth. Like a pearl," she said. "Thank you, Giles."

Giles filled her hands with shells. "You and Remember can use them for dishes when you play house," he said.

"You didn't forget to bring back the greens and the stick horses and these shells," she said. "You kept your promise, Giles. We've had Christmas after all."

An icy wind caught Damaris' shawl and blew it over her head. Drops of rain began to fall, faster and faster. They sounded like hail upon the deck.

"Hurry, we'll be soaked!" Giles cried.

They ran to the shelter of the companionway. In its safety, Giles stopped to let his sister catch her breath. He thought of the men left on shore. He hoped they could find shelter from the sleet and wind under the trees.

Suddenly he was thankful for this strong good ship. The creak of its timbers sounded friendly. The old smells of tar and turpentine and wood and wine were like friends, too. Here, he and Damaris and the other Pilgrims were safe.

If Captain Jones hadn't brought about a truce between the angry sailors and us, he thought, we'd all be ashore, shivering in this storm. Then he knew that the Pilgrims owed Captain Jones for much more than their Christmas cheer on the *Mayflower*.

As in Pilgrim Thanksgiving, *the people in this story are real, although the story is fiction based on historical facts. William Bradford wrote in his diary about this Christmas. "Munday, the 25th day [of December, 1620]. We wente on shore—some to fell timber, some to saw, some to rive, and some to carry, so no man rested all that day—*

"We wente to work on Plymouth's first building, the Common House, construction of which began on Christmas day."

In Pilgrim Reader, *George Willison says there was a little good cheer on Christmas night. Captain Jones invited all, Saints and Strangers alike, to share together, which all did to their content.*

And Bradford records: "So on boarde [Christmas night] we had diverse times, but those on shore, none at all. That night we had a sore storm of wind and raine."

*Captain Jones has never been given enough credit for his part in making possible the settlement of Plymouth. Due to delays in departing from England (September 16, 1620) and storms at sea, the May-*flower *reached the New World much later than planned. It was November 11 when she anchored off Cape Cod near where Provincetown now is.*

The Pilgrims explored the Cape and did not decide upon Plymouth as a home until Wednesday, December 20. On Thursday and Friday there were such severe storms no one could leave the ship. Saturday, men went ashore and chose sites on which to build. That night they left a guard of men on shore against possible attacks from Indians. Sunday the Pilgrims spent in worship. Monday, Christmas Day, was their first day of work on the new settlement.

For weeks the sailors had demanded a return to England before winter made the seas more dangerous and their food supplies gave out. Captain Jones would not leave until homes were built for the women and children. He stayed in the harbor so that the Pilgrims could live on the Mayflower while they worked on their houses.

Bradford records in his diary that the Bosun was a "prowd yonge man" who used to "curse & scofe at ye passengers." When Bradford was ill and asked for a certain food which the sailors had, he says the Bosun and his cronies mocked at him in his suffering and swore that "if he were their owne father, he should have none." Captain Jones heard of this, and said the Pilgrims should have what they needed "though he drunke water homeward bound."

ABOUT THE AUTHOR

While she was doing research for her first book, *Pilgrim Thanksgiving*, Mrs. Hays decided to write the story of the Pilgrims' Christmas on the *Mayflower*. She read in Bradford's diary that the Pilgrims laid the foundation for their Common House on Christmas Day, 1620; and she discovered the important role Captain Jones played in the Plymouth settlement by refusing to abandon his passengers until they had built adequate shelter on land.

After writing *The Story of Valentine*, when she proved a second time her gift in making history and legend come to life for children, Mrs. Hays returned to her characters, Giles and Damaris Hopkins, and wrote this lovely story of their first Christmas in the New World.

ABOUT THE ARTIST

Roger Duvoisin has written and illustrated many books of his own, and his imaginative drawings for *Christmas on the Mayflower* contribute greatly to the charm and character of the story.

Other Books by Wilma Pitchford Hays

HAWAIIAN WAY

ABE LINCOLN'S BIRTHDAY

EASTER FIRES

PILGRIM THANKSGIVING

THE STORY OF VALENTINE

FREEDOM

FOURTH OF JULY RAID

HIGHLAND HALLOWEEN

GEORGE WASHINGTON'S BIRTHDAYS